This book is dedicated to
my Dad, my Mom, Tammy,
Grandma Logan, Dawn, Sandy,
Sara, Bryan, Granny Parr,
The Ruggeras, and The Goins
Love, Todd

First Edition

Library of Congress Cataloging-in-Publication Data
Parr, Todd.
    The okay book / Todd Parr.
        p.   cm.
    Summary: In illustrations and brief text, enumerates a number of different
things that are okay, such as "It's okay to be short" and "It's okay to dream big."
    ISBN 0-316-69220-4
    [1. Self-esteem — Fiction. 2. Identity — Fiction.] I. Title.
PZ7.P24470k 1999
[E] — dc21   98-3283

10 9 8 7 6 5 4 3

TWP

Printed in Singapore

THE Okay Book

Todd Parr

Little, Brown and Company
Boston   New York   London

It's okay to be Short

It's okay to wear two different socks

It's okay to Eat all
the Frosting OFF
Your birthday Cake

It's okay to wear Glasses

It's okay to come from a different place

It's Okay to be Scared

It's Okay to wear what You Like

It's okay to Share

It's okay to cry

Boo   Hoo

It's okay to Live
in a Small HOUSE

It's Okay to have no Hair

It's okay to hang
out in the rain

It's Okay to be a different coLor

It's okay to
wear Braces

It's okay to put a
Fish in your Hair

It's okay to Dream BiG